DINO-BASEBALL

LISA WHEELER
ILLUSTRATIONS BY BARRY GOTT

 CAROLRHODA BOOKS MINNEAPOLIS · NEW YORK

AL'S TAIL WAX

For my son-in-law, Nick,
who gave my daughter, Kelly,
a perfect diamond.
—L.W.

For Rose, Finn, and Nandi
—B.G.

Text copyright © 2010 by Lisa Wheeler
Illustrations copyright © 2010 by Barry Gott

Carolrhoda Books
A division of Lerner Publishing Group, Inc.
241 First Avenue North
Minneapolis, MN 55401 U.S.A.

Website address: www.lernerbooks.com

Library of Congress Cataloging-in-Publication Data

Wheeler, Lisa, 1963–
        Dino-baseball / by Lisa Wheeler ; illustrated by Barry Gott.
             p.   cm.
        Summary: Meat-eating dinosaurs face plant-eating dinosaurs
in a baseball game.
        ISBN: 978-0-7613-4429-2 (lib. bdg. : alk. paper)
        [1. Stories in rhyme. 2. Dinosaurs—Fiction.
3. Baseball—Fiction.] I. Gott, Barry, ill. II. Title.
III. Title: Dinobaseball.
PZ8.3.W5668De 2010
[E]—dc22   2009020915

Manufactured in the United States of America
1 – DP – 12/15/2009

Jurassic Park . . . a perfect day.
Dino-Baseball's under way!

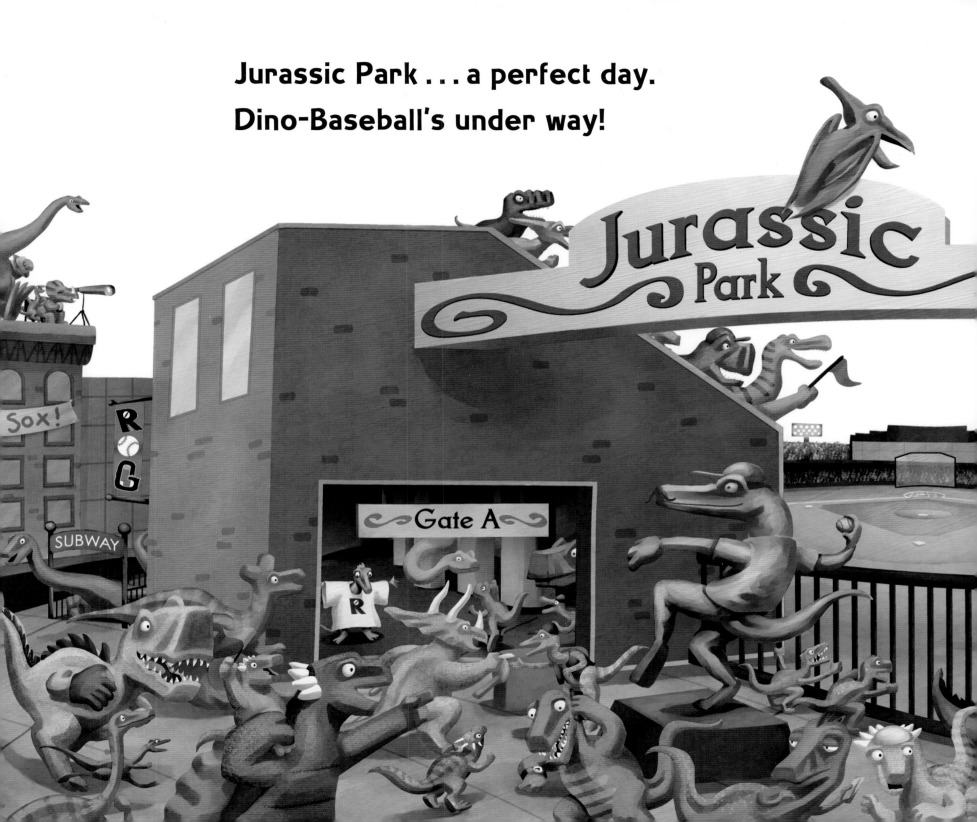

GREEN SOX
TRICERATOPS—PITCHER
IGUANODON—CATCHER
MAIASAURA—FIRST BASE
STEGOSAURUS—SECOND BASE
PACHYCEPHALOSAUR—THIRD BASE
LESOTHOSAURUS—SHORTSTOP
APATOSAURUS—RIGHT FIELD
DIPLODOCUS—LEFT FIELD
ANKYLOSAURUS—CENTER FIELD

RIB-EYE REDS
T. REX—PITCHER
TROODON—CATCHER
RAPTOR—FIRST BASE
ALLOSAURUS—SECOND BASE
GALLIMIMUS—THIRD BASE
COMPSOGNATHUS—SHORTSTOP
PTERODACTYL TWINS—
LEFT AND RIGHT FIELD
BARYONYX—CENTER FIELD

GREEN SOX host the **RIB-EYE REDS**—
Some pterosaurs, some quadrupeds.

Caps with brims shield midday sun.
Shoes with cleats help dinos run.

Wooden bats and leather mitts.
Warm-up throws and practice hits.

Hats on hearts as anthem plays.
T. rex cries while **Leso** sways.

First at bat is **Troodon**.

He taunts the pitcher, "Bring it on!"

The pitch is good. He swings with grace,
then hustles 'round to second base.

Tricera has an awesome grip.
A knuckle ball—he lets it rip!

Galli's swing's not up to par—
her hit just doesn't go that far.

Now watch that **Maiasaura** race!
Tags **Galli** out two yards from base.

A man on third, what happens next?
Strike out **Raptor**, then **T. rex!**

Four innings of a pitcher's duel.
Both teams are running out of fuel.

Three up, three down. No one scored.
Baseball fans are getting bored.

Then **Stegosaurus** for the **Sox**
hustles to the batter's box.

T. rex is the go-to guy.
Windup! Pivot! Let it fly!

As wood hits ball, they hear a *CRACK!*
A mighty swing has split the bat!

Stego rumbles down the line.
Compy calls, "This one is mine!"

Gloves the ball. Throws him out.
That's what baseball's all about!

But wait . . .
The **Green Sox** manager's irate,
throws his hat and kicks home plate.
He calls the ump a nasty name
and gets ejected from the game.

Then **Diplodocus** gets a hit.
Ankylo makes the best of it.
Pachy scores a home run play.
Three RBIs the **Green Sox** way!

Top of the sixth, **Sox**—3, **Ribs**—0.
But **Red team** fans are all aglow.

Bases loaded, **Green Sox** fret.
In the dugout, **Rib-Eyes** sweat.

Bary's up. His hit is sweet!
Rib-Eye runners move their feet.

The ball is headed toward the fans.
Diplo dashes to the stands.

Jumps up high, his glove held wide.
A **Sox** fan plucks it from the sky.
That home run makes the **Green Sox** cry,

"Whhhhyyy!"

Seventh inning stretch is here.

Green Sox fans sing songs and cheer.

Rib-Eye fans chomp meaty steaks.
They all line up for bathroom breaks.

It's 3 to 4—bottom of the eighth.
The **Green Sox** players don't lose faith.

They truly want to win this game,
and **Maia's** bat has perfect aim.

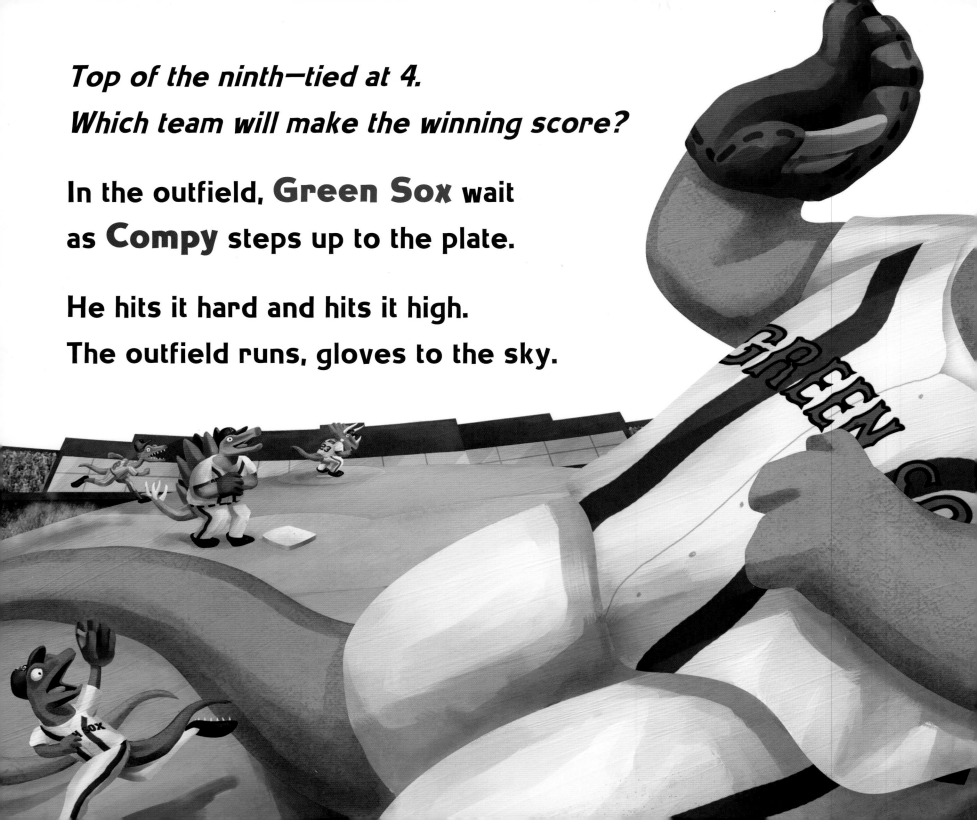

Top of the ninth—tied at 4.
Which team will make the winning score?

In the outfield, **Green Sox** wait
as **Compy** steps up to the plate.

He hits it hard and hits it high.
The outfield runs, gloves to the sky.

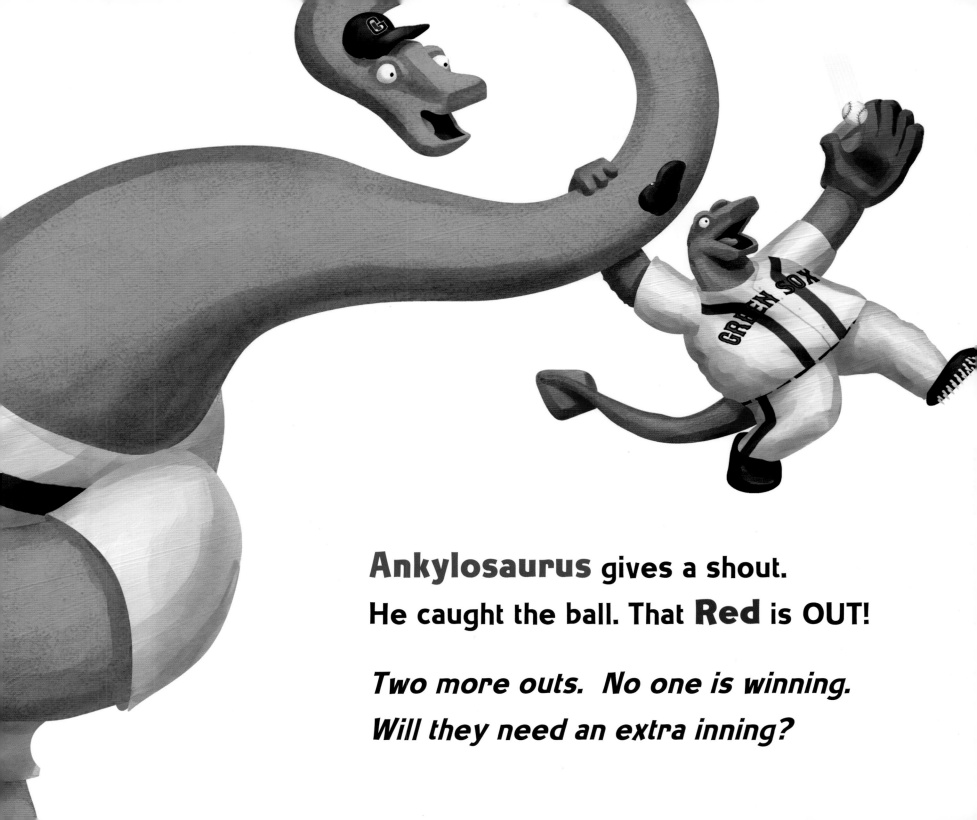

Ankylosaurus gives a shout.

He caught the ball. That **Red** is OUT!

Two more outs. No one is winning.

Will they need an extra inning?

Green Sox need to change the score.

Their only hope? **Apatosaur!**

He's at the plate. He sets his stance.

Strike one! Strike two! Just one more chance.

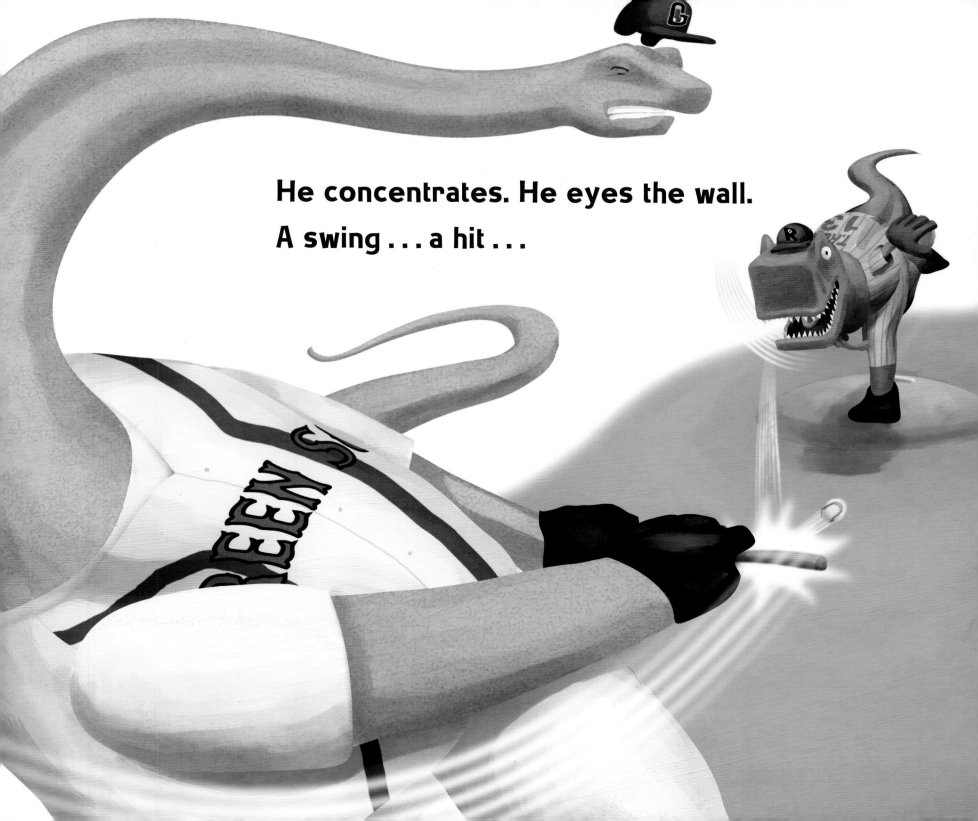

. . . and good-bye ball!

The Sox mascot jumps up and down.
Confetti's falling all around.

The crowd goes wild up in the stands.
The field is mobbed by Green Sox fans!

Buy your tickets at the court
for **Dino-Hoops**—next season's sport!